Earl felt a knot forming in the pit of his stomach. What if his class was still reading out loud? What if—just to punish him even more—Mrs. Mota asked him to try one more time?

His nerves made his bathroom problem even worse. He bounced up and down. "Do you guys think I'll get in trouble for going to the boys' room without permission?"

"Permission from who?" asked Maxie. "No one's even in charge of you right now. Your teacher thinks you're still in the principal's office. And the principal thinks you're back in your—"

Suddenly, Maxie stopped talking, and his eyes opened wide in amazement.

"Class," he heard himself say. "The principal thinks all of us are back in *class.*"

Earl bounced faster. "Yeah? So?"

"So don't you get it?" he asked. "Everyone thinks that we're someplace *else.* No one is looking for us. It means we could…"

He looked all around, then lowered his voice to a whisper.

"…*leave school.*"

Kids love Barbara Park's books so much, they've given them all these awards:

Alabama's Emphasis on Reading

Arizona Young Readers' Award

Charlotte Award (New York State)

Dorothy Canfield Fisher Children's Book Award (Vermont)

Flicker Tale Children's Book Award (North Dakota)

Georgia Children's Book Award

Golden Archer Award (Wisconsin)

Great Stone Face Award (New Hampshire)

Iowa Children's Choice Award

IRA-CBC Children's Choice

IRA Young Adults' Choice

Junior Book Award (South Carolina)

Library of Congress Book of the Year

Maud Hart Lovelace Award (Minnesota)

Milner Award (Georgia)

Nevada Young Readers' Award

North Dakota Children's Choice Award

Nutmeg Children's Book Award (Connecticut)

OMAR Award (Indiana)

Parents' Choice Award

Rebecca Caudill Young Readers' Book Award (Illinois)

Rhode Island Children's Book Award

Sasquatch Reading Award of Washington State

School Library Journal's Best Children's Book of the Year

Tennessee Children's Choice Book Award

Texas Bluebonnet Award

Utah Children's Book Award

West Virginia Honor Book

William Allen White Children's Book Award (Kansas)

Young Hoosier Book Award (Indiana)

The GEEK CHRONICLES

Maxie, Rosie, and Earl—Partners in Grime

The GEEK CHRONICLES

Maxie, Rosie,
and Earl—
Partners
in Grime

Barbara Park

SCHOLASTIC INC.

New York   Toronto   London   Auckland   Sydney
Mexico City   New Delhi   Hong Kong   Buenos Aires

ISBN 0-439-35643-1

Text copyright © 1990 by Barbara Park.
Cover art copyright © 2000 by Peter Van Ryzin.
All rights reserved.
Published by Scholastic Inc., 555 Broadway, New York, NY 10012,
by arrangement with Random House Children's Books,
a division of Random House, Inc.
SCHOLASTIC and associated logos are trademarks and/or
registered trademarks of Scholastic Inc.

12 11 10 9 8 7 6 5 4 3 2 1   2 3 4 5 6 7/0

Printed in the U.S.A.   40

First Scholastic printing, January 2002

* CONTENTS *

THE GEEK CHRONICLES 1:

Maxie, Rosie, and Earl—Partners in Grime

1 EARL

Earl Wilber sat at his desk and doodled on the back of his reading workbook. The class was reading a social studies assignment out loud, but Earl wasn't sure what it was about. His doodle was taking all of his concentration. He was drawing a cartoon of a monster's foot crushing his new school.

Fifth grade wasn't fun. Not when you were a new kid. Not when you had no friends.

Earl had hated Dooley Elementary from the very beginning. As he walked across the playground on the first day of school, two girls ran by and called him Plumpy.

You big stupids! thought Earl. He didn't say it out loud, though. Earl was only brave in his head.

He had never made friends easily. Not only

was he shy, but new situations made him tense and sweaty. And whenever Earl was tense and sweaty, he almost always did something dumb. Like when it was his turn to stand at his desk and introduce himself to his new classmates, he had clicked his heels and saluted like a soldier. He still didn't know why.

"You're trying too hard," his mother had told him when she drove him to school the next morning. Then she handed him a Kleenex to wipe the sweat from his top lip.

"Just be yourself, Earl. If you just relax and settle down, you'll have new friends in no time."

But, of course, Earl knew that wasn't true. Friends didn't flock around you just because you were all limp and relaxed. And besides, trying to act limp and relaxed made Earl tense.

It's not like he hadn't tried to make friends. Last Tuesday at lunch, he had tapped Anthony Jabbort on the arm and offered him half of his cream-filled cupcake. But Anthony had just wrinkled up his nose and said, "Gross. You've had your mouth all over it."

Things didn't get any better that day, either. Later that same afternoon, Mrs. Mota had asked Earl to read out loud in front of the entire class. They had been reading a story about a boy and his sailboat. Earl had been following along when suddenly he heard his name called.

"Earl Wilber? Would you read the next paragraph for us, please?"

Shocked, he looked up. What was she calling on him for? He hadn't raised his hand, had he?

"Earl?" said Mrs. Mota again. "We're waiting."

Earl's heart started pounding like crazy. He was terrible at reading out loud. He always got tongue-tied. Always.

Nervously, he glanced down at the sentence.

With a gust of wind at his back, little John sailed, himself.

Okay. It didn't seem that hard, really. It was simple, in fact. Maybe if he took a couple of deep breaths, he could get through it.

He wiped the moisture off his forehead and began.

"'With a gust of wind at his back...little John soiled himself.'"

The classroom exploded with laughter. Even Mrs. Mota couldn't keep the corners of her mouth from turning up.

"Sailed!" he yelled quickly. "I mean little John sailed, himself!"

But the laughter was too loud for anyone to hear. And Earl Wilber had wanted to die.

From that moment on, he decided he would never read out loud again. Which is why, on this particular day, as the class was reading a social studies assignment, Earl was drawing a monster's foot stepping on the school.

"Earl?"

Oh no. No way. It *couldn't* be. Not again.

As he raised his head, Mrs. Mota was smiling directly at him. "Could you take a turn reading, please, Earl?" she asked.

He couldn't believe it! Why did she keep doing this to him? What had he ever done to make her hate him so much?

The silence in the room was deadly. Earl's collar felt tight around his neck. He stretched it out so he could breathe.

"Page twenty-two, paragraph three," the teacher said.

Earl tried to look at his book, but the memory of what had happened the last time was still too fresh in his mind.

"We're waiting, Earl," Mrs. Mota told him. "I'd really appreciate it if you would just give it a try again. I know you can do it."

Earl shook his head no. He hadn't really planned on shaking his head no. It was just sort of happening on its own.

Mrs. Mota raised her eyebrows.

"Excuse me, Earl?" she said. "Are you saying you won't read? Are you telling me *no?*"

This time, Earl's head bobbed yes. It's like it was on automatic pilot or something.

The next thing he knew, Mrs. Mota was out of her chair and walking toward him. As Earl watched her coming, a little whimper escaped from his throat.

Go back! Please! he wanted to holler. I'll read!

I'll read! But even though he opened his mouth to speak, nothing came out.

A second later, Mrs. Mota was standing over him, glaring down at his doodle. She tapped her foot.

Panicking, Earl picked up the paper and shoved it into her hands. "Here," he blurted stupidly. "I made this for you."

Mrs. Mota helped him out of his chair. "I'm sorry, Earl, but I think you'd better come with me."

She held him by the hand and led him out the door. His palm was so sweaty, it slipped from her grasp.

"I don't know what it was like at your last school, Earl," she said, "but at Dooley Elementary, we don't tell the teacher no. Maybe you'll understand our rules better if Mr. Shivers explains them to you in person."

That's when it finally hit him. Earl didn't know why it had taken him so long. But it wasn't until that exact second that he realized Mrs. Mota was taking him to the *principal's office!*

Frantically, he grabbed hold of her sweater.

"No! Please! I can't go there! My mother will kill me!"

But Mrs. Mota kept right on walking.

"I'm sorry, I'm sorry!" said Earl. "I changed my mind! I'll read now! I'll read!"

They passed a poster hanging on the wall. "COME TO THE ICE CREAM SOCIAL!" he read as loudly as he could. "Look, see? I'm reading!"

Mrs. Mota's expression softened a little. "I'm sorry, Earl. Really, I am. But I honestly think Mr. Shivers can help you with your attitude."

With each step toward the office, Earl's legs got weaker. His skin felt hot and cold at the same time.

He fanned himself. "I think I might be having a heart attack," he said. But Mrs. Mota paid no attention.

When they got to the office, she opened the door and led Earl inside. The secretary, Mrs. Trumbull, looked at Earl like he was a criminal.

He fanned himself some more. "Could you call an ambulance, do you think?" he asked her.

Mrs. Trumbull pointed to a yellow plastic

chair on the other side of the counter and told him to take a seat.

Earl walked to the corner and slumped down in the chair.

"Mr. Shivers is very busy right now," Mrs. Trumbull told his teacher. "It could be quite a while before he's able to talk to your boy over there."

"That's okay," said Mrs. Mota. "I don't think it will hurt Earl to sit there for a while. He's got plenty to think about."

Mrs. Trumbull craned her neck to see him. "Do you ride the bus, young man?"

Earl shook his head no.

"Good. Then there's no problem," she told Mrs. Mota. "If Mr. Shivers can't see him till the end of school, we'll just dismiss him from here."

"That'll be just fine," said Mrs. Mota.

She glanced at Earl one last time and left the office.

The principal's door was closed. A small sign hung on the doorknob. It said: THE PRINCIPAL IS YOUR PAL.

Earl squeezed his eyes shut. He sat there like that for a very long time, it seemed. Then, all of a sudden, the door opened and Mr. Shivers rushed into the room. He was tall and bald and wore a bright green suit.

Earl gulped. What kind of man would buy a suit like that? A *weird* man...a *dangerous* man.

Earl trembled. An *insane* man.

Mr. Shivers and the secretary whispered back and forth a minute. Then Mr. Shivers sighed tiredly and looked over at him.

"Mr. Wilber? You want to step into my office a minute?" he said. "I'm very short of time, but I'll try to squeeze you in."

Earl thought he should reply, but the spit in his mouth had dried up and his lips were stuck together.

When he went inside the office, Mr. Shivers offered him a seat.

As Earl sat down, he felt his top lip start to quiver. He tried to get it to stop, but he couldn't. It was a lip out of control.

"My secretary told me that Mrs. Mota brought

you down to talk to me," said Mr. Shivers. "Is that correct?"

Earl covered his quivering lip with his hand and opened his fingers slightly. "Is it warm in here to you?" he asked quietly.

Mr. Shivers sat down. "Tell me why you're here, son," he said.

Earl wanted to cooperate, but he just couldn't think straight. It was as if his brain had completely shut down.

"Why am I here? Why am I here?" he repeated stupidly to himself.

Then, for no reason at all, he let out a giggle. He'd heard of people cracking up in times of stress, and now it was happening to him. Nothing was funny. Nothing at all. But Earl giggled again and again.

Stop it! his brain ordered him. This isn't funny! Now shut up and tell Mr. Shivers what happened before it's too late.

He took a shaky breath. "Well, um, let's see…the class was reading a social studies page out loud…and, well, I didn't actually want to get called on today...so I guess maybe I was... *doodling*."

Doodling. As soon as the word was out of his mouth, Earl Wilber started to laugh. Doodle. Had it always been that funny? Doodle, doodle, doodle!

Earl tried to get control of himself, but it was no use. He finally collapsed in a wild fit of hysterics. It was the sloppy kind of laughing, too, the kind with lots of nose snorts and pig snuffles. He tried muffling his mouth with both hands, but the noises exploded through all ten of his fingers— which made him laugh even louder.

Earl pulled his shirt up over his face so the principal couldn't see the tears running down his cheeks.

Mr. Shivers stared at Earl's stomach and waited for him to quiet down. It seemed to take forever before the boy's hysterics began to taper off.

"Hah, hah, hah, hah...hee, hee...hah...heh, heh, heh...aaahhhh."

"Finished?" Mr. Shivers asked him at last.

Earl took a deep breath and nodded his head.

"Good," said the principal. "Then why don't you go back outside for a few minutes. We'll talk again when you're completely settled."

Earl dabbed his eyes with his shirt one last time and pulled it back down where it belonged. Shakily, he stood up and hurried out the door past Mr. Shivers.

As he scrambled back into the yellow plastic chair in the waiting room, the secretary peered at him over her typewriter.

Feeling sicker than ever, Earl Wilber slumped down and out of view.

2 ROSIE

Earlier that morning, Rosie Swanson's class had been taking their weekly spelling test. After listening carefully to each word, Rosie would print it neatly on her paper, then quickly spread her arms across the answers, so no one else could see.

Even though nobody sat directly next to Rosie, Judith Topper sat in front of her. And with Judith Topper around, there was always a chance of cheating.

Judith was the worst speller in the room. She was always the first one to sit down during a spelling bee. Once, just to be nice, Mr. Jolly had asked her to spell the word *a*. Judith spelled it "e." On the way to her seat, she said she thought it had been a trick question.

In the front of the room, Mr. Jolly smiled. *"Urgent,"* he said, loud and clear. "The last spelling word today is *urgent.*"

Rosie pushed her red-framed glasses back up on her nose and ran her fingers through her wispy blond hair. Her bangs were too long, but she liked them that way. When your bangs were too long, you could look at people through your hair and they never knew they were being watched.

When Rosie was sure that the coast was clear, she uncovered her test paper and printed URGENT in space number ten. She smiled. Another 100 percent, she thought proudly as she turned the paper facedown on her desk.

In front of her, Judith Topper began to squirm in her chair. A second later, she dropped her pencil on the floor and leaned down to pick it up. As soon as she was out of the teacher's view, Judith strained her neck to look at the paper of the girl in front of her.

After she saw the word she needed, Judith sat back up and printed it on her test.

Rosie was infuriated. Nothing made her angrier

than cheating. It just wasn't fair! Why should she spend her time studying for these stupid spelling tests when cheaters like Judith ended up with the exact same grade?

Rosie cupped her hands around her mouth. "I sawwww youuuu, Judith," she whispered in the cheater's ear.

But instead of erasing the word she'd stolen, Judith turned halfway around in her chair and called Rosie a not-so-nice name.

Okay, fine. That did it. Rosie pulled out the little yellow notepad she kept hidden in her desk and printed clearly:

> Dear Mr. J.
> Judith T. cheated on her spelling test again this week.
> Sincerely yours,
> R.S.

Rosie folded the note as small as she could and pressed it into the palm of her hand. After that, she grabbed a pencil and headed for the pencil sharpener. As she passed Mr. Jolly's desk, she dropped the note into his center drawer.

Rosie smiled to herself. She was good at this tattletale business. She really was.

The rest of the class was lining up for lunch. Rosie sharpened her pencil and went back to her desk to grab her lunch sack. She was just on her way out the door when she heard her name called.

"Miss Swanson? Could you come back here, please? I need to speak to you a minute."

Mr. Jolly was sitting at his desk. Rosie made a smooth U-turn and headed back in the door. She liked being called Miss Swanson. It made her feel grown-up.

Mr. Jolly waited for everyone to leave. Then he reached way back into his top drawer and pulled out several little yellow notes. Rosie watched him smooth each one and stack them on his desktop.

"I'm sorry to keep you from your lunch, Rosie," he said, "but I'm afraid I have to speak to you about these notes again. I was hoping that our talk last week was going to put an end to the tattling. But since then, you've written this many more."

Rosie pushed her red glasses up on her nose and leaned in for a closer look.

"Did you get the one I just put in there a minute ago? The one about you-know-who cheating on her you-know-what?"

Mr. Jolly didn't reply. Instead, he picked up the stack of notes and began to read:

> Dear Mr. J.
> Michael P. was in the girls' bathroom.
> Your helpful student,
> R.S.

Rosie nodded. "Yes, sir. And I don't think it was an *accident,* either, if you get my drift."

Mr. Jolly looked at her for a few seconds.

"Note number two," he said.

> Dear Mr. J.
> At lunch, Mona Snyder chewed

up her ham salad sandwich and opened
her mouth and showed everybody.
Your eyes in the lunchroom,
R.S.

Rosie made a sick face. "It was so gross
I couldn't eat my raisin cookie after that," she
said.

Mr. Jolly went on:

Dear Mr. J.
Ronald M. blew his nose in
the drinking fountain.
Yours sincerely,
R.S.

This time, Rosie cringed. "And you understand that he didn't use a Kleenex, right, sir? He
just held this one nostril closed and blew out of
the other one."

She paused. "I believe it's called a farmer's
blow."

Mr. Jolly held up his hand. "Please. I don't

need the details, okay? In fact, I didn't need to know any of these things at all."

Rosie stretched her neck to see into the drawer. "Yes. But you still haven't gotten to the one about you-know-who cheating on her you-know-what."

Mr. Jolly rubbed his temples. "Rosie, last week didn't I ask you to stop all of this tattling? Wouldn't you rather spend the day enjoying your classmates rather than sneaking around like a little spy all the time?"

Rosie didn't even have to think about it. "Not really, sir. Actually, I like the sneaking around part."

Her teacher sighed. "But you're in fourth grade now, Rosie," he said. "You can't keep tattling for the rest of your life."

This was the part Rosie just didn't get. "But how can you stop all the bad stuff that's going on if you don't know about it, Mr. Jolly? You can't be everywhere, you know? I'm helping."

Mr. Jolly shook his head. "I know that you *think* you're helping, Rosie. But tattling on every little thing that goes on in this room is not the way to get along with people. What's going to happen when they find out what you're doing?"

"But they *won't* find out, Mr. Jolly," she insisted. "I'm seriously good at this. My grandfather was a police detective. Sneaky is in my blood."

Why did she have to keep explaining this stuff—especially to an adult who should understand?

"Telling on people isn't really *bad,* you know," she said. "I'm doing it for their own good. Like if a burglar gets caught by the police, he gets punished and he learns his lesson. But if he never gets caught, he keeps stealing from people forever, probably. I'm telling you, Mr. Jolly, if we nip Judith's cheating in the bud, we can steer her straight."

Mr. Jolly's headache was getting worse. "Look, Rosie. I agree that kids sometimes get away with stuff they shouldn't. And sometimes, it really is your duty to report things that you've seen. But you're carrying this thing way too far. There's very little that I won't find out eventually.

And in the meantime, if you need to report on something, save it for important things. Things that are seriously dangerous or against the law."

"Like?" she asked.

Mr. Jolly grinned a little bit. "Like if Judith Topper finds out you've tattled and she whacks you in the head with her thermos at lunch, you can tell me, okay?"

Rosie frowned. "Assaults at the lunch table are not a laughing matter, sir. Last year John Paul Rice hit a kid in the head with a frozen banana on a stick, and he almost knocked the kid out. It sounds funny maybe, but it wasn't."

Mr. Jolly stopped smiling and stood up. "I was making a joke, Rosie. All I want you to do is use better judgment and ease up on the notes, okay?"

Rosie said okay and left for lunch.

Mr. Jolly took two aspirin and headed for the teacher's lounge for a bowl of soup. An hour and a half later, when his class returned from lunch and PE, he was feeling much better.

Rosie Swanson strolled in the door. Mr. Jolly looked up and gave her a wink.

Rosie smiled. Then, much to his surprise, she walked over to his desk, pulled a piece of napkin out of her pocket, and dropped it in his desk drawer.

The note read:

Dear Mr. J.
During lunch, Mona S. tried to poke my eye out with a carrot.
Reporting danger,
R.S.

Five minutes later, Rosie Swanson was sitting in a yellow plastic chair outside the principal's door.

Next to her, a plump, sweaty kid was slumped over in his seat.

3 MAXIE

Rosie peeked at Earl through her bangs. She hadn't expected him to be looking back at her.

The boy wiped sweat off his lip.

"I'm not well," he said.

Rosie moved down a seat.

On the other side of the school, Maxie Zuckerman's temper was about to boil over. The afternoon in Mrs. Trout's fifth-grade class had started out badly and gotten worse and worse. Lunch had been okay, but when he'd returned to the room, Mrs. Trout had been passing back yesterday's math tests.

Maxie knew what he was in for. He was a "Z" name. And when your class was seated in alphabetical order like his was, "Z" names always sat in the last desk of the last row. That meant when papers were passed back, everyone in the row got to see Maxie's test grades before he did.

Kids were never nice about it, either. This time, David Underwood was the first to start mocking him.

"Big surprise. Maxie Zuckerman got another perfect paper," he said.

David leaned his head out into the row and looked back. "Get a life, why don't you, *Dork*erman?"

David passed the test paper to Melissa Waterman. She called him Maxie Geekerman and passed it on.

Maxie's muscles tightened. As usual, their teasing was getting to him.

"Just hand it back," he said.

By now, the test was in the hands of Daniel Wieczkiewicz. Or, as he was better known, Daniel "W."

Daniel W. sat at the desk right in front of

Maxie's. It was another unfortunate consequence of being seated in alphabetical order.

As soon as Daniel W. got Maxie's paper, he spun around in his seat and grinned. There was chocolate milk on his mouth from lunch.

"Here you go, Brainiac. Another perfect paper to take home to Mumsy and Poopsy. They'll be so proud."

Daniel W. dangled the paper in front of him. Maxie grabbed for it. He knew that Daniel would only pull it away, but he never stopped trying.

"Give it here, Daniel! I mean it!"

"Man, it must be terrible being you," said Daniel. "Don't you ever wish you were normal like the rest of us?"

Maxie crossed his arms. "I don't know, Dan. Would I have to wear milk on my face like you?"

Quickly, Daniel W. wiped his mouth. Then he crumpled the test paper into a ball and dropped it on the floor next to Maxie's foot.

"You niblick," Maxie mouthed.

"Hey. Watch your mouth," said Daniel. But Maxie just smiled. Words were almost always his best weapons. It was amazing how upset kids got when they didn't know what they were being called. Just like now, when he was only calling Daniel a golf club.

He leaned over and picked his test paper off the floor. If only Mrs. Trout had moved his seat to the front of the room like he'd asked her to do, stuff like this wouldn't keep happening. Alphabetical order was so unfair. Not only did he have to sit behind the jerkiest kid in the room, but in his heart, Maxie knew he could be a class leader. And leaders had to be in *front* of people, not behind them. Leaders had to be in the *spotlight*. But every time he asked to move, his teacher's answer was always the same.

"Sorry, kiddo," Mrs. Trout would say. "No can do."

"Yes, Mrs. Trout. *Yes* can do," he told her the last time they talked. "How would you like it if every time you made an A on a test or a report, the whole row started making fun of you?"

Mrs. Trout put her hand on his shoulder. "Maxie, my dear boy, you're such a smart kid. Why don't you realize that the kids only tease you because they see how much it bothers you. If you'd laugh it off a few times, they'd stop. I promise."

Maxie rolled his eyes. "I laugh when things are funny, Mrs. Trout. And these kids are trying to be mean. They do lots of mean stuff. Like last week when you handed back our history papers, someone made a hat out of my Hats of the World report. And yesterday when you handed out new reading workbooks, mine had this little booger or something on the cover."

Mrs. Trout made a face. "Please, Max. Enough. No matter where I put people, there are going to be complaints. Alphabetical order is the best thing I've found so far. And unless there's a medical reason why you can't sit in the back, you're in the back."

She walked Maxie to the door. "See you tomorrow," she said.

When he didn't leave, she nudged him into the hall and locked the door behind him.

"But I wasn't finished yet!" he called. "I still have issues!"

Mrs. Trout didn't come back.

Finally, Maxie Zuckerman stomped his foot and stormed home.

The memory of that conversation was still clear in his head as Maxie uncrumpled his math test. More than anything, he wanted to squeal on Daniel W. and the others for teasing him again. But in fifth grade, you had to be careful who you snitched on. In addition to being the brainiest kid in the room, Maxie was also the scrawniest. And scrawny snitches didn't last long on the playground.

He was still stewing over things when someone knocked on the classroom door. Seconds later, Mr. Bucky, the traveling art teacher, came into the room. He was pulling his work cart behind him. Until this year, Mr. Bucky had always had his own art room. But because the school was overcrowded, they had turned the art room into a new third grade during the summer. And it had put Mr. Bucky into a permanent bad mood.

Mrs. Trout clapped her hands to get everyone's attention. "Time for art! Time for Mr. Bucky!" she announced loudly. "Put your books away, people, and clear your desks."

The art teacher looked especially tired today. He stooped over slowly and pulled a pile of black paper from the bottom shelf of his cart.

"Columbus Day is coming up in a couple of weeks, so we're going to make sailing vessels," he said dully. "I've got black paper for the bottoms, and white for the sails. Questions?"

Just to be annoying, Daniel W. asked, "What's a vessel?"

Vanessa Wainwright shot her hand in the air. "I know! I know! My father's a doctor. So I happen to know that vessels are little tubular things that carry blood around your body."

Maxie let out a groan. Stupid comments like that drove him crazy.

"Yeah, real good, Vanessa," he said. "Christopher Columbus sailed to America in a blood vessel."

Daniel W. spun around in his seat. "Are you saying he didn't, Mr. Brain? How do you know,

Mr. Brain? Were you there, Mr. Brain?"

In the front of the room, Mr. Bucky was going from row to row, counting out paper. When he got to Maxie's row, he looked at the few sheets in his hand and sighed.

"Sorry, but there's not enough black paper left," he said. "Someone will have to use another color."

Daniel W. grinned meanly. "Gee, I wonder who that will be?"

As the construction paper headed back, there were four pieces of black paper and one piece of...pink. *Pink?* No way! thought Maxie. Any color but pink!

As soon as Daniel W. put it on his desk, Maxie grabbed the pink paper and went flying to the front of the room.

"No, Mr. Bucky. Come on. I'll use any other color for my ship except this," he said. "A pink ship is just plain stupid."

Mr. Bucky looked annoyed. "This is my third class in a row, okay? Pink is all I have left. Deal with it."

Maxie stood there a second, wondering what to do next. When nothing came to mind, he headed back to his seat. That's when he noticed that Daniel W. was at the pencil sharpener.

Yes! This was his chance!

In a flash, he snatched Daniel's black paper off his desk. When Daniel W. came back, Maxie was hunched over the black paper, guarding it with his life.

"Hey! Hey! He stole my paper!" Daniel hollered.

Within seconds, the art teacher came storming down the aisle.

Quickly, Maxie bolted out of his seat and gave the black paper back to Daniel W.

"Kidding! I was just kidding, Mr. Bucky. I wasn't going to keep it. I swear. It was a joke."

The teacher pointed his finger in Maxie's face, forever it seemed. Finally, he went back to the front of the room.

Maxie sat down at his desk again. When the scissors were passed back, he got the rusty ones.

For the rest of the period, Mr. Bucky showed the class how to fold, cut, and staple the construction paper into sailing vessels. For Maxie, each step of working on his ship got more and more humiliating. Christopher Columbus wouldn't have been caught dead on a ship like this—not even if Queen Isabella had said, "Pink is all I've got left. Deal with it."

Across the room, Carlton Bagget accidentally ripped his paper. When Mr. Bucky offered him pink paper, Carlton walked back to his seat empty-handed.

"Just give me an F," he said.

Finally, the hour was almost up. Mr. Bucky held his ship in the air and gave his final instructions. "Before you staple on the sails, I want each of you to write the name of your ship across the bottom of the sail in clear black letters. You have three names to choose from. Who knows what they are?"

Once again, Vanessa Wainwright's hand rocketed into the air. "The *Niña,* the *Pinta,* and the *Santa María,*" she called out. "I know those because last year we did a play, and I was the *Santa María.*"

Suddenly, Daniel W. whipped around and snatched Maxie's ship off the top of his desk. "Wait! We forgot one!" he hollered.

He held Maxie's ship over his head for everyone to see. "What about *The Little Pinkie?*"

Maxie grabbed for his ship, but he couldn't reach it.

Daniel W. sailed it all around in the air. "A lot of people don't know this, but *The Little Pinkie* brought all the flamingos to the New World."

Everyone started to laugh.

"You fuff," Maxie muttered angrily. It only meant "puff." But it would have made Daniel W. mad, probably—if he hadn't been laughing so hard, that is.

Finally, Mrs. Trout stepped in and made the class quiet down. Daniel W. tossed *The Little Pinkie* over his shoulder. It landed on the floor again, next to Maxie's foot.

That's when Maxie Zuckerman's temper finally boiled over. Without even thinking about it, he picked up his rusty scissors, grabbed a loose wad of Daniel's army T-shirt, and cut a hole.

Daniel felt the tug and spun around. Calmly, Maxie spread the small piece of camouflage-colored material on top of his desk.

"Oh dear," he said quietly. "My scissors slipped."

At 1:45 P.M., Maxie Zuckerman was sitting outside the principal's office.

A plump kid was lying limp on the seat to his right.

On his left, a skinny girl with glasses was staring at him through her bangs.

4 NOT FAIR, NOT FAIR, NOT FAIR!

Earl Wilber, Rosie Swanson, and Maxie Zuckerman glanced at each other out of the corners of their eyes. Twice, Maxie and Earl caught each other looking and quickly turned away.

Rosie had seen Maxie before, but the pudgy one was definitely a new kid. She still couldn't believe she was sitting here. In a huff, she took off her glasses and cleaned them on her skirt. How could Mr. Jolly have done this to her? He told her to report dangerous situations, hadn't he? And vegetables weren't exactly *harmless*, you know. Just last month a little kid in her neighborhood got a butter bean stuck up his nose, and his grandma had to call the paramedics.

Maxie Zuckerman was just as upset as Rosie.

Not fair, not fair, not fair! he thought. If Mrs. Trout had moved me to the front of the room, none of this would have happened. It's *her* fault I'm here, not mine! She's the one who pushed me over the edge. Mrs. Trout and that stupid Daniel W.

"Not fair," he said right out loud.

Earl sat up in his chair. "Huh? What?" He was hoping that the skinny kid was talking to him. But when Maxie ignored him, Earl slouched back down again. In addition to all his other problems, now he had to go to the boys' room. He tried shifting positions, but it didn't help much.

After a few minutes, Mr. Shivers' secretary came out of the principal's office. "I'm sorry," she told the three of them, "but Mr. Shivers just received another important phone call, so he's going to be a while longer. You'll just need to sit here and behave yourselves until he can see you."

"But I shouldn't even *be* here," Rosie told her. "I didn't do anything wrong. I promise."

"Neither did I," said Maxie. "This isn't fair. I watch *Judge Judy*. And I'm telling you, this definitely isn't fair."

Rosie's ears perked up at the mention of her favorite television show. She leaned over toward the skinny kid. "Did you see the one where that man was suing some little kid for throwing a rock at his windshield?" she whispered. "Only it turned out not to be a rock at all. It turned out to be a small jar of—"

"Shh," said the secretary.

Rosie lowered her voice even more. "Cheez Whiz."

"Shh," hissed the secretary again.

After that, they sat there for more than ten minutes before Mr. Shivers came hurrying out his door.

Rosie stared at his green suit. "Our pal looks like a green bean," she said to no one in particular.

Her comment made Earl bust out laughing again. He'd tried to hold it in, but it exploded right out of his mouth.

Mr. Shivers turned his head. "Still haven't been able to put a lid on it, have you, son?" he said.

The principal grabbed a folder off the counter

and headed for the outside door. "Sorry, troops," he told them, "but I've got to leave for the rest of the day. Looks like you people have lucked out for now. You can go back to your rooms, but I expect to see each of you here bright and early Monday morning."

Then, without another word, the door closed, and he was gone.

For a second, Maxie, Rosie, and Earl just sat there. They were stunned, almost. Things like this only happened in movies and books. In real life, kids *never* got off this easy.

Slowly, Maxie stood up. It was a miracle! That's what it was! He stretched his arms out to the sky. "Thank you, God," he said. "Thank you, thank you. You did the right thing here. I mean it. You did."

Just then, he felt Mrs. Trumbull's hand on his shoulder. She spun him around.

"You're the Zuckerman kid, aren't you? It's Maxie, isn't it? You *do* understand the part about coming back on Monday morning, don't you, Maxie?"

Maxie nodded, but he wasn't worried at all. Monday was three days away. And anything could happen in three days. Mrs. Trout could change her mind and realize the whole scissors incident had been her fault. Or maybe on Monday morning, Mr. Shivers' windshield would be hit by a small jar of Cheez Whiz on his way to school. The important thing was that, for the moment, Maxie's prayers had been answered.

After she gave them their hall passes, Mrs. Trumbull led them into the hall. "Go back to class," she said sternly. Then she turned and she went back into the office.

Still not believing their own good luck, the three of them stood in the hall, frozen almost. Then finally, they relaxed a little, and they started to walk.

Maxie had only gone a few steps when he stopped again. No, wait. Hold it. Go back to his room? Back to all those smirking faces? You had to be kidding!

"I *can't*," he said out loud. "The kids in my room will laugh their heads off if I go back now.

You guys don't know the kind of mungos I've got to face back there."

Rosie wondered what a mungo was, but she had her own problems to deal with. How could she face all the stares from her classmates? All her life, she'd tried to set such a good example for the other children. And now they would think she was bad like them.

"And I didn't even *do* anything," she said.

Earl felt a knot forming in the pit of his stomach. What if his class was still reading out loud? What if—just to punish him—Mrs. Mota asked him to try one more time?

His nerves made his bathroom problem even worse. He bounced up and down. "Do you guys think I'll get in trouble for going to the boys' room without permission?"

"Permission from who?" asked Maxie. "No one's even in charge of you right now. Your teacher thinks you're still in the principal's office. And the principal thinks you're back in your—"

Suddenly, Maxie stopped talking. His eyes opened wide in amazement.

"*Class*," he heard himself say. "The principal thinks all of us are back in *class*."

Earl bounced faster. "Yeah? So?"

"So don't you get it?" he asked. "Everyone thinks that we're someplace *else*. No one is looking for us. It means we could…"

He looked all around, then lowered his voice to a whisper.

"…*leave*."

Earl froze again. For a second, Rosie did, too. Then suddenly—almost violently—she began shaking her head. Oh no. No way! Where was her notepad? The Zuckerman kid was actually talking about ditching school!

"That's nuts!" she sputtered. "Leaving school is illegal. It's completely against the rules." She pulled off her glasses again and nervously wiped them on her skirt. But as she did, her eyes sneaked a peek at the big exit doors down the hall.

Next to her, Earl Wilber's brain was in chaos. Leave? Just leave? Oh geez…if only he could! If only his mother wouldn't find out!

The boys' room was across the hall, and he had to go worse than ever.

"Wait for me!" he told Maxie. "Please. I mean it! Don't go anywhere without me. I'll be right back."

Maxie looked at his watch. Could he really do this? Even if it was completely foolproof, cutting school would take guts. The guts of a *leader*.

Rosie was watching every move he made. "You're not serious about this, are you?"

"Why not?" asked Maxie. "It's my teacher's fault that all this happened. And besides, Mrs. Trout thinks I'm being dismissed from the office. So who's going to know?"

Rosie screamed inside her head, Me! I'm going to know, that's who! And I'll have to tell on you, too! I won't want to, but I'll have to.

Maxie looked at his watch again. The seconds were ticking away. Go or stay, go or stay? He had to make a decision before another teacher came along and found them in the hall.

"I'm going for it!" he said. "I'm outta here!"

Just then the boys' room door opened, and Earl came running over.

"Come on! We're leaving!" Maxie said excitedly.

Rosie backed up from them. "Oh no, we're not. Not *me*. I can't. I really, really can't."

Maxie grabbed Earl's arm and started down the hall. Earl's legs felt like jelly.

"My mother's going to kill me," he said shakily.

"No, she won't. Your mother's not even going to know. Do you think I'd be doing this if I thought my parents would find out? I'm not crazy, you know."

Rosie ran up behind them.

"You guys are going to get caught," she said. "I'm telling you the truth. You're going to get suspended for this."

Maxie looked at the boy beside him and shook his head. "No, we're not, are we...uh, what was your name again?"

"Earl. Earl Wilber."

"Are we, Earl Wilber?"

Earl smiled a little bit. School had started three weeks ago, and this was the first kid who had called him by his name.

The two boys took off running toward the exit doors.

Rosie gasped.

She couldn't let them get away with this!

She just *couldn't!*

5 GRIME CITY

Maxie hit the exit doors with a thud. He'd expected them to fly open. But instead, the locked doors threw him backward.

He hit Earl in the stomach.

"OOOMPH," said Earl, and the two of them fell to the floor.

They had just gotten up when the second-grade teacher, Mrs. Conklin, stuck her head into the hall.

Thinking fast, Maxie threw his arm around Earl's shoulder. "Dodgeball accident," he blurted. "We're on our way to the nurse."

Earl was still hugging his stomach. "Auuggh," he groaned.

Mrs. Conklin's eyes glanced down the hall at

Rosie, who was pretending to get a drink of water.

"Let's be on our way, people," called the teacher to all three.

Doubled over, Earl began to shuffle away. As soon as Mrs. Conklin shut her door, Maxie grabbed him by the arm again and pulled him around the corner. There were more exit doors at the end of the next hall.

They were almost there when Emily Sweete came skipping out of the girls' bathroom in front of them. Maxie had to sidestep to keep from knocking her down.

Emily checked to make sure she was okay. She smoothed out her new red dress and adjusted her name tag. Even though her teacher, Mrs. Petrie, had learned her name weeks ago, Emily still liked wearing the name tag to school. When everyone knew your name, it meant that you were famous.

She watched closely as the two boys stopped at the big doors and looked back at her. They seemed to be in a hurry, Emily thought. The little one kept looking at his watch, and the big one was fidgeting.

Emily Sweete fluffed her hair and started skipping toward them. She had just learned to skip two days ago, but already she was one of the "best little skippers in the world." Grammie and Poppie had even said so.

Earl watched in horror as the little girl got closer. "She's coming! She's coming!" He grabbed Maxie's shirt. "Why is she coming?"

Maxie was as upset as Earl. Please, little girl. Go back, go back, he begged silently.

But Emily kept on skipping. She loved the way her stiff crinolines made her dress bounce up and down. When she got to the doors, she twirled around in a circle, then stopped right in front of them.

"I can skip," she said. "I just learned."

Frantically, Earl pulled the bottom of his shirt up over his face so she couldn't see him.

Emily stared at his bare stomach and pointed. "That boy's zipper is down," she said to Maxie.

Maxie stooped next to her. "I have an idea, Emily. Why don't you skip back to your room, and we'll watch you, okay?"

47

Emily smoothed out her dress. "Okay," she said. "Only first I have to rest for a second. 'Cause I don't want to get perspiration on me."

She leaned over and checked to make sure her lacy socks were still in place. Sometimes when she skipped, they slipped down inside her shoes.

"Please," begged Maxie. "Just go, okay? Earl and I are waiting."

Earl hit Maxie on the arm. What a stupid mistake to tell the girl his name!

"My name's not Earl!" he said. "It's…it's Ted."

By now, Emily Sweete was ready to skip again. "Okay, here I go. Watch me, Ted. Watch me!"

She waited until Earl lowered his shirt enough to see out. Then she started skipping from side to side in a fancy zigzag pattern.

When she was almost back to her classroom, she turned her head to smile at her two admirers.

But her audience was already gone.

Maxie took off across the parking lot. Earl was close behind. Too close. He stepped on Maxie's heel and pulled off his shoe.

"Hey! My shoe! My shoe!" Maxie yelled.

"Run in your sock!" hollered Earl as he passed him.

Annoyed, Maxie ran back, grabbed the shoe, then sped forward. He ducked behind the first car he came to. Earl was already there. He was on his back, trying to slide under.

Maxie grabbed his leg. "Hey! Where are you going?"

"We've got to hide!" called Earl. "That little girl saw our faces! She's going to squeal on us, I'm telling you! They'll be looking for us any minute!"

Maxie rolled his eyes. This kid was turning out to be a total loon.

"Quit acting like a slub, Earl. We've got to keep moving. If we don't keep moving, we'll get caught for—"

Before he could finish his sentence, they heard the school doors come flying open again.

"See? I *told* you!" cried Earl. In a panic, he tried to sit up. But he clunked his head on the car's muffler and went back down with a thud.

Maxie peeked around the tire to see who was coming.

Rosie Swanson dove beside him on the ground. "I came to get you! You have to come back! You have to!" she said.

"Oh no. No way," Maxie told her. He pointed to the school gate. "Look how close we are to freedom. We're not going back now, are we, Earl?"

Earl wiggled out from under the car. His clothes were covered with splotches of grease and he was rubbing the bump on his head.

"You called me a slub," he said, offended.

Maxie's eyes scanned the parking lot. "Never mind that. We've got to make a break for it. I don't think we should run at the same time, though. It's too risky."

Just then, he spotted the school Dumpster. "See that giant trash bin down there?" he said. "I'll run down there and hide behind it. Then, when it's safe for you to come, too, I'll give you the all-clear signal."

Maxie stood up and swung his arm in big, full circles at his side. "See this, Earl? See what I'm doing? This will be the all-clear signal."

Rosie smirked. "That's not an all-clear signal," she said. "That's what guys at the airport do to show the planes where to land."

Maxie narrowed his eyes. "Oh really, Miss Know-It-All? Well, for your information, it's also going to be an all-clear signal."

Rosie glared at him. "Good. Fine. Suit yourself. But don't blame me if a plane lands on you."

Maxie looked at the Dumpster one more time. His stomach was churning like crazy. Just do it! he ordered himself. Just go!

Almost on their own, his feet took off across the parking lot. Faster! Faster! he told himself. Don't stop! Don't look back!

Behind him, he could feel the other two watching his back. For once in his life, all eyes were on him. Maxie Zuckerman was the man! Maxie Zuckerman was in the *spotlight!*

He was almost to the Dumpster now. Just a little way to go.

That's when he heard it. Pounding footsteps coming up behind him! He was being chased!

He pulled in his shoulders, ducked his head, and ran faster.

In a flash, the girl from the principal's office blitzed past him.

And after her came Earl Wilber.

"No, you guys! No! *I'm* supposed to be the leader, not you! Go back and wait for the all-clear signal!" Maxie hollered.

But neither Rosie nor Earl slowed down until they reached the Dumpster.

Disgusted, Maxie stopped and walked the last few feet.

Behind the Dumpster, Earl was huffing and puffing and holding his heart. "You big dummy!" he snapped at Rosie. "You said someone was coming! But there wasn't."

Rosie grabbed Earl by the shirt. "Watch who you're calling dummy, *dummy*," she growled. "The name is Rosie Swanson. And for your information, I thought I heard voices."

When she finally let go, Earl smoothed out his collar. "Same to you, fella," he sputtered stupidly.

Maxie threw his hands in the air. "Knock it off,

you two! We don't have time for this! Look how close the gate is now. Come on. We'll just walk out real calm, like we're not doing anything wrong."

"No! I'm not going, I told you," said Rosie. "I came out to get you guys. But there's no way that I'm going to walk out that—"

CLANG! CLANG! CLANG!

The sudden noise of the school bell made Rosie scream. "Oh no! They found us! They found us! It's an escape siren! Just like in those prison movies!"

She grabbed Earl and ducked behind him to hide.

"Quit it! Let go of my shirt! You're stretching it!" Earl growled. He tried to swat her away.

Maxie shouted at them both. "It's not an escape siren! It's a fire drill! We've got to hide, you guys! They're going to come pouring out of the school any second."

He ran to the nearest car door and tried to open it. Locked!

Desperately, he looked back at the Dumpster. His eyes opened wide. Of *course!* The answer to their problem was staring him right in the face!

"Quick! In here!" he called. And without another word, Maxie Zuckerman took a huge leap, kicked his foot over the edge, and went over the top of the trash bin.

Rosie and Earl watched as his head disappeared out of view.

A second later, it appeared again. "Hurry up! Get in!" he ordered.

Earl held his nose and made a sick face. Stinky places made him woozy.

"Give me a break!" Maxie yelled back. "It's almost empty! And besides, what choice do you have? You either get in here or you get expelled.

"NOW!" Maxie shrieked.

Earl was shocked into action. He tried to kick his leg over the side of the can, but it wouldn't reach, and he fell back down.

"I can't do it! I can't! I'm a dead man! I'm dead!" he said.

Rosie couldn't wait one more second. "Out of my way!" she yelled. She made a flying leap over the top of the Dumpster and landed safely inside.

Just then, the school doors opened, and kids started pouring into the parking lot.

Earl gave it one last try. This time, he kicked his leg as hard as he could. His foot caught on the edge of the bin, and he tumbled in on top of Maxie and Rosie.

The three of them hit the bottom of the can with a bang. Rosie's glasses fell off. When she grabbed for them, her hand hit something slimy.

"Sick!" she said disgustedly. She wiped whatever it was on her new yellow skirt. "Sick, sick, sick!"

Earl held his nose as tight as he could. "I tan't breeeathe in here. It tinkt too bad!"

"Shh!" hissed Maxie. "If anyone hears us, we're toast!"

Within seconds, commotion and noise were all around them. Maxie, Rosie, and Earl crouched in terror and prayed that no teacher would look over the edge.

They waited and waited. Fire drills were supposed to be speedy, but this one seemed to last forever.

Outside the Dumpster, two impatient kindergarten girls began tapping on the side of the can like a drum. Another little boy started kicking it. Harder and harder and harder.

Rosie held her head. The banging was giving her a headache. If she ever made it out of here alive, she would find the little nitwit who was kicking the can and report him to Mr. Jim, the head custodian. The custodian who hated kids.

Out in the parking lot, Hannah Marshall had just been caught chewing gum.

"Dispose of it *immediately*," her teacher ordered.

Embarrassed, Hannah walked to the side of the big can and spit her gum into her hand. Then, wanting to make sure she didn't miss, she flung it over the top with all her might.

Earl felt something hit his arm. A bug, maybe? A little raindrop? As he looked closer, his mouth fell open in digust. The gum was stuck to the hair on his arm. When he tried to flick it off, it stuck to his fingernail. Hoping not to gag, he finally scraped it on the side of his shoe.

Maxie's eyes kept darting around the top of

the Dumpster. Please, just don't let a teacher's head appear. Please, please, please. Finally, he squeezed his eyes shut. Maybe—if you really, really didn't want to see something—it was better not to look.

Earl felt dizzier than ever. What if he had a heart attack in here? What a terrible place to croak. Instead of going to heaven, he'd be carted off to the dump, where he'd have to lie around with a bunch of old refrigerators.

Finally, the bell stopped its loud clanging. Maxie, Rosie, and Earl listened as everyone began to trample back into the building.

They looked at each other hopefully. Was it possible? Could they *really* be out of danger?

The parking lot was quiet for a very long time before anyone in the Dumpster had the nerve to move.

Maxie was the first one to his feet.

He stood on his tiptoes and peeked over the top. There was no one in sight at all.

He turned to the others and raised his fist in victory.

Seconds later, Maxie Zuckerman, Rosie Swanson, and Earl Wilber climbed out of the Dumpster.

They ran like the wind.

6 ZUCKERMAN NUMBER TEN

Earl Wilber drank Pepto-Bismol for breakfast. He put a bowl and a spoon in the sink to fool his mother into thinking he had eaten. But the thought of food made him sick.

It was 9:30 on Saturday morning. Earl had been trying to find Maxie Zuckerman's number in the phone book for thirty minutes. So far, he had dialed nine different numbers and gotten nine wrong Zuckermans. Only four of them had been polite enough to say good-bye.

Earl looked at the next number on the page. This one *had* to be the one. It just had to. He picked up the receiver.

"Earl? What are you doing in there?" Mrs. Wilber shouted from her bathroom. "Are you on the phone? Who are you calling?"

Earl rolled his eyes. His mother had the biggest ears in the universe. They didn't look that big. But even when she was in the shower with the door closed, she could hear what he was doing.

It was spooky having a mother like that. One time she heard him sneaking a bowl of chocolate pudding all the way from Mrs. Martin's house next door. She'd called him on the phone and said, "Put it back."

Quickly, Earl put the receiver back down. "No one! I'm not calling anyone!" he yelled back. Geez! The next thing he knew, she'd be peeking around corners with a periscope.

He waited for her to turn on the shower. Then he slid the kitchen door closed and tried one more time. Zuckerman number ten.

"Please be the one. Please. Please," he begged.

It rang three times before someone answered. "Hello?"

Earl lowered his voice to a hush. "Hello, is Maxie there?" he said.

At first, there was no reply.

"Why? Who is this?" said the voice finally.

Earl's heart beat faster. "I need to speak to Maxie Zuckerman. Is this him? Is it you, Maxie?" he asked.

"Yeah, okay, fine. It's me. Now who is this? Mr. Whispers?"

Relieved, Earl cupped his hand around his mouth.

"No. It's me. It's Earl Wilber. You know. The kid from the Dumpster yesterday."

On the other end of the phone, Maxie frowned. "Earl? What's wrong with your voice? Why are you talking so soft?"

Earl listened for his mother again. "Wait a second. Hold on," he said.

Then, just to be sure she wasn't lurking somewhere, he went into the living room and checked behind the couch and chairs. When he was sure it was safe, he went back into the kitchen.

"Maxie? You still there?" he asked.

"Yeah, but why are you acting so weird? What's going on?"

Earl swallowed hard. The news he was about to give Maxie was not good. He'd been trying to put it out of his mind. But now he finally had to say the words out loud. A shiver went through his body.

"Someone *saw* us."

Maxie's blood went cold. For a second, he couldn't breathe.

"No," he gasped. "No way."

"Yes way," Earl said back. "I *saw* him, Maxie. I saw him see us."

This time, there was no response at all.

"Are you still there?" asked Earl. "Don't you want to know who it was?"

Earl waited a few more seconds, then blurted it out.

"*Mr. Jim*, Maxie! It was Mr. Jim!"

Maxie groaned. He'd been trying to brace himself. But the news was worse than he thought.

He closed his eyes. "Are you sure, Earl? Are you positive it was Mr. Jim? The custodian who hates kids? The one with the bleeding dragon tattoo on his arm?"

Earl nodded. "Yup. That's the guy. He was coming around the corner with his bucket with the wheels on it, and he saw me fall out of the Dumpster. You and Rosie were already running for the gate. But he saw all of us. I know he did. I wanted to holler at you guys, but I couldn't exactly scream out your names. So I just took off running, and I didn't stop till I got home."

By this time, all the color had drained out of Maxie's face.

"But you're totally positive it was Mr. Jim, right? Was he wearing black high-tops? And did his bucket have a skull and crossbones painted on the side?"

Earl shivered again. "It was him, Max. I swear. What are we going to do?"

Maxie put the phone down on the kitchen table and laid his head next to his cereal bowl. He knew Earl was still there, but he needed to think.

Outside, Maxie's father was mowing the lawn. Maxie could see him between the slats of the mini-blinds. Just looking at his father made him uneasy. Mr. Zuckerman was not a reasonable man about things like this. They would *never* look back on this and laugh, for example.

On the other end of the line, Earl Wilber was going crazy.

"Psst! Maxie! Maxie! Are you still there? Come on! Answer me! Oh geez, you didn't hang up, did you?"

Maxie could hear Earl blabbering. The kid was driving him crazy. He picked up the phone. "For crying out loud, Earl! Give me a second here, would you? Would you just give me a second? I've gotta think!"

"Yeah, well, while you're thinking, maybe I should call that girl Rosie," said Earl. "Maybe she can help us figure out what to do. We need to get our stories straight. That's important, don't you think? That we all tell the same story?"

Maxie was still staring out the window at his dad. For some reason, his father looked bigger than he used to. Could he have grown? Had he been working out?

"Geez, Maxie. Say something. Don't just keep me hanging on like this," Earl said. "The three of us should meet somewhere and come up with a story. It's important."

He paused for a second to listen for his mother. "We can't meet here, though. That's for sure. My mother has these gigantic ears you wouldn't believe. I mean, they look normal, but—"

Maxie didn't hear the rest. Mr. Zuckerman had just come in the kitchen door.

"Dad! Hi! Hi, Dad!" Maxie blurted, way too loudly.

Calm down! he ordered himself. Act normal!

Maxie took a deep breath. "Been mowin' the lawn, Dad?" He glanced out the door. "Yeah, you've been mowin', all right. Hot out there today? You need a drink of water?"

Mr. Zuckerman looked at his son oddly. "Are you feeling okay?" he asked.

"Me? Oh yeah. Sure. I'm fine, Dad. Fine, fine, fine." He held the receiver out to show his father. "I'm just sitting here talking to my friend Earl."

"Ted!" yelled Earl. "Call me Ted!"

Maxie was more flustered than ever. "I mean Ted...Earl Ted...my good friend Earl Ted."

He put the phone back to his ear. "So…how are you doing today, Earl Ted?"

Mr. Zuckerman got a drink and went back outside.

Maxie felt sicker than ever. Why had he acted so insane? His father didn't believe a word he was saying. He had to pull himself together.

"I need to call you back," he told Earl. "I think I just had a mental breakdown or something."

"No!" Earl hollered. "You can't hang up yet! We've got to set up a meeting. We have to, Maxie! I'll bring Rosie. Just tell me where to meet."

Maxie's head had started to pound. "Okay, okay. We'll meet behind my garage at noon. It's the yellow house across from the junior high. I'll see you then."

After that, the line went dead.

Earl put his mouth closer. "Hello? Hello? Maxie?" He called into the receiver. But there wasn't a sound.

When Earl finally hung up, he sat back in his chair and took some deep breaths. At least now he wasn't alone with the terrible news. At least now there was someone who felt just as sick as he did.

He sat there a few minutes longer. Then he walked to the sink and took another swig of Pepto-Bismol.

7 EXCUSES, EXCUSES

Rosie Swanson left her house at 11:45 A.M. and headed for the yellow house across from the junior high. It had been two hours since she'd gotten the phone call from Earl.

Rosie wasn't used to spending the afternoon with kids her own age. When she was little, she used to play with other kids all the time. But sooner or later, she almost always had to tattle on them for their own good. And now she hardly got invited anywhere.

This time, though, she wasn't going anywhere to play. This time it was serious. *Very* serious. She still didn't know why she'd let herself chase those two boys into the parking lot yesterday. Her grandfather had warned her over and over that people who broke the rules got caught.

One time when she visited him at the police station, he even showed her an actual criminal being fingerprinted. His name was Lloyd Boyd, and he'd stolen an old lady's purse. Lloyd Boyd said he'd only been looking for a hankie. But even though his nose was running, no one believed him.

Rosie was almost to Maxie's now. His house was just across the street from where she stood. She stopped at the school crosswalk and looked both ways to see if any cars were coming.

That's when she spotted the jaywalker. It was a boy, she thought. And he was wearing a hooded Eskimo parka and a ski mask.

Rosie adjusted her glasses. She couldn't be sure, but for some strange reason she thought it might be…

"Earl?" she hollered. "Hey, Earl Wilber! Is that you?"

The kid in the parka tensed up for a second. Then he pulled the hood of the big jacket down even farther over his forehead and ran across the street.

Rosie ran after him. "Hey! Stop! Wait for me, Earl! Wait up!"

The kid didn't stop running until he was behind Maxie's garage. Then, huffing and puffing, he pulled off the wool ski mask and threw it on the ground.

Earl's face was red from running. His eyes looked tired and bloodshot. "Great! Perfect! Scream my name to the whole world, why don't you?" he snapped.

Just then, Maxie yanked open the back door of the garage and pulled them both inside. "Shh! Be quiet!" he growled. "Do you want my father to hear you?"

But as soon as the door was closed again, Earl kept right on yelling at Rosie. "Why would you shout out my name like that? Huh? You totally blew my cover!"

Normally, Earl was not an aggressive person, but his disguise had been very important to him. After all, sneaking the old moth-eaten fur parka out of the house without being seen had not been easy. It had to be moved in stages. First, from the attic to the laundry room. Then, from the laundry room to behind the sofa. And then finally, out the back door and behind the bushes.

It had been worth it, though. Not one person who saw him walking to Maxie's that morning could have identified him. At least, not until Rosie the big-mouth had started blaring his name all over the universe.

Rosie wasn't bothered by Earl's anger at all. She crossed her arms and stared at him. "I don't get this. What's the big deal about saying your name? In fact, why were you wearing a disguise in the first place?"

Earl hesitated. Sweat drops from his forehead were making wet spots on the garage floor.

"Um, well, it's not a disguise, exactly," he said finally. "It's more like...a costume, sort of. I just felt like dressing like an Eskimo today. What's wrong with that?"

"Maybe nothing," said Maxie. "But if that's all you were doing, why didn't you want Rosie to say your name?"

Nervously, Earl began rocking back and forth

on his feet. Maybe it would be better just to tell them the truth and get it over with.

"Let's just say it sort of went through my mind that I shouldn't be seen with you guys, that's all," he said.

Rosie frowned. "Why? How come?"

Earl stretched out the neck of his shirt so he could breathe easier. "Because you two have gone to this school since kindergarten, right? So I bet you anything Mr. Jim knows *exactly* who you are. But as for me...well, you know..."

He forced a sick smile. "I'm a new kid."

"Yeah, but you said that Mr. Jim saw your face," said Maxie.

"He did," said Earl. "But only for a second. And I'm positive he doesn't know my name."

Just then, a light went on in Maxie's brain. "Oh, *I* get it now," he growled. "Just in case all three of us get caught, you're here to get your story straight. But if it turns out that Mr. Jim can only identify Rosie and me, you're going to let us take all the blame."

Earl reached into his pocket and pulled out a

pack of Rolaids. "Is it warm in here to you?" he asked.

Rosie and Maxie were disgusted. What kind of a kid was Earl Wilber, anyway? What sort of person would just look out for himself and not care what happened to anyone else?

They were both about to let him have it when Earl spoke up.

"Of course there's another side to this, you know," he said. "Maybe *I'll* be the only one caught. Who knows? Maybe Mr. Jim didn't actually see your faces, so he won't be able to identify you at all. But he saw mine for sure. I'm positive of that much."

He narrowed his eyes at Maxie. "So what will you do if that happens, huh? If I'm the only one who gets caught, are you and Rosie going to come running into the office and tell Mr. Shivers that you were in the Dumpster with me?"

Maxie and Rosie looked at each other. They never actually answered the question, though. Everyone already knew the answer.

Finally, Maxie sighed and pointed to an old

car parked in the garage. "Let's sit in there," he said. "It's more private."

The car was a '55 Chevy. Its paint job was chipped in spots, and it was resting on four flat tires. Maxie opened the back door and motioned for Rosie and Earl to get inside. After they were settled, he looked out the garage window to make sure his father wasn't nearby. Then he got on his knees on the front seat and faced them.

"Okay, you guys. I know we're all worried about Mr. Jim seeing us. But he's not the only person who knows we left school. There's also that little foozle who saw us in the hall. That little fub with the name tag. Emily something or other."

"Sweete," Earl said quickly. "Emily Sweete. Daughter of Vincent Sweete. She lives on North Lily Lane. Phone number: 555-2215."

Maxie's eyes opened wide. "How did you know that? Did you call her, Earl? Oh my gosh. What did you say?"

Earl squirmed uncomfortably in his seat. While he'd been making phone calls that morning, he thought he could take care of the Emily problem, too. But it hadn't worked out exactly the way he'd planned.

"Um, well...I thought that maybe if I scared her a little, she wouldn't squeal on us. So I told her that I was the bogeyman. And I said that if she told anyone about the two boys in the hall on Friday, I'd be paying her a little visit."

Maxie looked excited. "Yes! Way to go, Earl, baby!" he said. "And so what did Emily say? Did she promise to keep her mouth shut?"

Earl turned his head and stared out the car window. It was obvious that he didn't want to answer.

"Earrrrrl! Come on. Tell us. Was she scared of you? What did she say?"

Earl folded his hands in his lap and stared down at them. He cleared his throat.

"She said if I came to her house, I could watch her skip."

Rosie groaned. "Oh no. I *told* you this would happen. I should never have come outside to get you. Now I'm in just as much trouble as you are, and I didn't even do anything."

Maxie glared at her. "Listen, you. It doesn't help to keep throwing that in our faces, okay? You could have gone back to the school any time you wanted to, but you didn't. You hid in the Dumpster and cut class just like us. So I don't care if you never did one wrong thing in your whole entire life…you've done one now."

Rosie didn't like to be scolded. She hid behind her hands and stuck out her tongue.

Maxie went on. "Unless we can come up with a good excuse for why we hid in the Dumpster and ran away, we're all going to get suspended. Now come on, you guys. Let's put on our thinking caps and figure a way out of this mess."

Earl put on his ski mask and began to think.

Except for the sound of breathing, the car was totally quiet.

"Think, people. Think, think, think," Maxie urged.

A few minutes later, Earl clapped his hands together. "I've got it! I've got an excuse for why we left school! My mother used it one time when she got caught for speeding, and the cop didn't even give her a ticket!"

Rosie nodded hopefully. "Yeah? So? What did she tell him?"

Earl looked at her through the two round eyeholes in the ski mask. "She told him that she had a chicken potpie in the oven," he said excitedly.

Maxie and Rosie stared at him for a very long time.

"That's it?" Rosie asked finally. "That's the excuse? You want us to tell Mr. Shivers that we had to leave school because we had a chicken potpie in the oven?"

Instantly, Earl felt like an idiot. Why did things always sound so good in his mind but so stupid out loud? Without saying another word, he took off his thinking cap and threw it on the floor.

Maxie sighed. "Okay, maybe we're just making it too complicated. Why don't we just keep it simple and tell Mr. Shivers it was all just a big mistake."

Rosie frowned a little. "We climbed into the Dumpster by mistake?"

"Yes," said Maxie. "Remember when we left the office and Mrs. Trumbull said, 'Go back to class'? We'll tell Mr. Shivers we thought she said, 'Go sit in the trash.'"

Once again, the car was filled with silence. When Maxie looked up, Rosie was staring a hole right through his head.

"Brilliant," she said.

Trying to maintain his dignity, Maxie slid down the seat and out of view.

In the corner, Earl was already digging around in his pocket again. He offered Rosie a Rolaid. She put it in her mouth, then opened the car door and spit it on the garage floor. Now that she was a criminal, spitting didn't bother her that much.

"What about this?" she said. "What if we offered Mr. Jim money not to squeal on us?"

"Money?" Earl asked.

"Yeah, you know. *Hush* money. Hush money is when you pay people not to tattle. We could put it in a big envelope and stick it in his mailbox with a note."

Earl shrank down. He didn't have any money.

He'd just spent his allowance on a digital ther-
mometer and a pair of Odor-Eaters.

Maxie pulled some lint out of his pocket and
put the fuzz in Rosie's hand. "That's it. That's as
much money as I have."

Rosie moaned. "Great. I don't have any
money, either. That means on Monday morning
we're going to get suspended. And it will stay
on our permanent record forever and ever. And
we won't be able to go to college. Or get a job. And
the next thing you know, we'll be stealing purses
from old ladies and saying we just needed a
hankie."

Earl started to panic. "No, no. Come on, you
guys. We can't just give up. Please. What if we call
Mr. Jim? What if we call him and beg him not to
tell? What if we—"

Tap, tap, tap.

Earl looked outside his window. Oh no! There
was a man there!

Trying to escape before he was seen, Earl
lifted up on the door handle and pushed with all
his might. Unfortunately, at that same moment,

Mr. Zuckerman opened the door from the outside, and Earl Wilber fell onto the garage floor.

Maxie hurried out of the car. Rosie did, too. How long had Mr. Zuckerman been standing there? Had he been listening? How much had he heard?

Maxie started to babble. "Dad! Hi! Hello! Hello, Dad! Hi!"

He pointed. "These are my, uh…well, friends. This is Rosie Swanson. And that one is—"

They looked down at the floor.

"Earl."

"Ted," said Earl.

"Earl Ted," said Maxie.

Mr. Zuckerman kept on standing there.

"It's okay that we're sitting in the car, isn't it, Dad?" Maxie asked. Not waiting for an answer, he turned to Rosie. "This was my dad's car when he was in high school. It almost still runs, too, right, Dad? All it needs are some new tires, a little body-work, a paint job, and an engine."

Maxie patted the hood. "Yessiree. This is what you call a classic car. It's a collector's item.

Not many of these babies around anymore, right, Dad?"

Mr. Zuckerman looked at Maxie oddly again. Then—still not saying a word—he stepped over Earl, grabbed a rake off the wall, and left.

Angrily, Earl jumped up and began dusting himself off.

"Thank you very much," he snapped at Maxie. "Thank you for not warning me that your father was opening my door. Thank you for letting me make a total fool of myself."

He reached into the car and grabbed his fur parka and ski mask from the floor. Then he put the heavy jacket on again and started for the door.

Maxie grabbed his arm. "No, Earl. Don't go home, okay? I mean it. Why do you have to go?"

Rosie grinned. "Maybe he has an Eskimo Pie in the oven," she said.

Just then, Maxie and Rosie looked at each other and busted out laughing.

Earl wanted to die. Why were people always laughing at him? Why was everyone so mean?

He tried to pull away from Maxie's grip, but

now Rosie had grabbed ahold of him, too. Even though she was still giggling, she was trying to apologize.

"I'm sorry, Earl. Really. I was only making a joke. I swear," she said.

"She *was*," said Maxie. "Come on, Earl. It was just funny, that's all. Can't you see that it was funny?"

With both of them pulling on his arms, Earl finally stopped struggling. He stared down at the floor and shuffled his feet a little.

Maxie gave him a pat on the back. "Stay," he said. "Please."

Earl took a big breath.

The three of them got back in the car.

8 COMING IN FOR A LANDING

By Sunday night, Maxie, Rosie, and Earl had still not come up with a plan. Depressed and nervous about what would happen the next day, they decided to meet on the school playground at 7:30 in the morning for one last try. Earl agreed not to wear a disguise.

When they arrived, it was hard to tell which of them looked worst. Rosie and Maxie were tired and pale. Earl was wearing big sunglasses.

"It's not a disguise," he said right away. "My eyes are red and puffy from not sleeping. And I didn't want my mother to start asking a bunch of questions. So I told her it was 'Sunglasses Day.'"

He burped quietly. "Sorry, but I couldn't keep my breakfast down, either. I mean, it went down okay. But it came right back up again. It was only half a bowl of Frosted Flakes, but still it—"

Maxie covered his ears. "Okay, okay. You don't need to paint us a picture."

Rosie sat on the swing right next to Maxie. Her hair was stringier than usual, and her eyes looked saggy.

"It's all over," she whined. "Ten years of being perfect, right down the toilet. By this afternoon, I'll probably be blowing my nose in the water fountain."

Maxie looked at his watch: 7:46. The bell would ring in forty-four minutes. The moment of doom was closing in.

"I know Mr. Shivers found out what we did," Rosie continued. "Mr. Jim probably called him as soon as he got home on Friday afternoon and blabbed the whole thing. That's always the best time to squeal on people, you know. While the incident is still fresh in your mind."

She paused a second, then added, "At least that's what I've been told."

Maxie closed his eyes. "I feel like I'm going to my own funeral."

Earl took his hand away from his mouth long enough to mutter, "You are."

Just then, Mr. Jim came around the corner of the school. He was carrying a load of paper towels into the office.

The three ducked down. Maxie hated this. The pressure was killing him. He had to get it over with.

Suddenly, he stood up and started walking toward the office. "I don't care if Mr. Jim sees me or not. If I don't get this talk with Mr. Shivers over right now, I'm going to go crazy. I mean it. I am."

He walked several steps, then turned around. "Well? You're not going to make me go in there alone, are you? You guys are coming, too, right?"

He lowered his voice a little. "Please?"

Rosie took a deep breath, then walked over next to him.

Both of them waited for Earl. When he didn't come, they went back and helped him up from the swing. Then, side by side, the three began the scary walk toward Mr. Shivers' office.

They were almost there when Earl collapsed in the grass and refused to get up again.

Rosie glared down at him. Now was *not* the time for Earl to pull another lame stunt.

She bent down and made a fist. "If you don't stand up, I'm going to hurt you," she said.

Earl got up and walked the rest of the way in silence.

When they reached the office, Rosie opened the door, and the three of them stepped inside. Mrs. Trumbull looked up from her desk. "Well, well, well. Look who's back," she said. Then she buzzed the principal in his office and went back to her work.

Within seconds, Mr. Shivers appeared in his doorway. He was wearing a black suit with a black tie and black shoes. Black, as in funeral director.

He rubbed his hands together. "Good morning, all. Glad to see everyone showed up this morning. Who would like to come in first?"

Maxie took a step backward. Thank goodness Zuckerman started with Z.

"How 'bout you, Mr. Zuckerman?"

Maxie gulped. What? How could this be?

"But…but I'm a *Z*," he said.

The principal smiled and nodded. Then he ushered Maxie into his office.

After the door was closed, Mr. Shivers sat on the edge of his desk and crossed his arms. "Okay, Mr. Zuckerman. Let's get right to the heart of the matter, shall we? I know what happened on Friday, okay? I've been informed about the whole episode."

Maxie gulped. "Informed?"

"Yes," said Mr. Shivers.

"Informed, as in 'squealed on'?" Maxie asked again.

"Well, I suppose you could put it that way," said Mr. Shivers. "The point is, I know what you did, Max. But that doesn't mean that I don't want to hear your side of things."

All morning, Maxie had been trying to be brave. But by now, it seemed as if all of his courage had evaporated into thin air.

Mr. Shivers tapped his foot. "We don't have all day, Mr. Zuckerman. Could you tell me your side, please?"

Maxie's voice sounded weak. "Well, I guess I don't really have a side, Mr. Shivers. I mean, I tried to think of a side, but nothing really sounded believable. So all I can say is that I was just really, really mad on Friday. And I didn't use good judgment. And, well, you know...I did what I did."

He thought a second, then added, "I'm only ten."

Mr. Shivers raised his eyebrows. "Anything else?"

Maxie felt desperate. "Love your tie."

Mr. Shivers couldn't help smiling. The smile didn't change anything, though. "You understand that I'm going to have to call your parents, right?" he said.

Maxie nodded. "Yes, but could you do me one little favor, please? Could you tell my dad that when he comes to pick me up that I'll meet him in the parking lot? I just don't want him to come storming into my classroom and carry me out over his shoulders like Andy Reilly's father did last year."

Mr. Shivers looked confused.

"But Andy Reilly was suspended, Mr. Zuckerman. Andy played hooky for three days. That's a little more serious than cutting someone's shirt with your art scissors, don't you think? Not that that was okay, but I don't think your father will be coming to get you."

Maxie frowned. Hold on a second. What was going on here? All this time, had Mr. Shivers been talking about the *shirt* thing? He hadn't been talking about the *Dumpster* thing?

The principal continued. "As I was saying, I'm going to call your parents today. And I will definitely expect you to buy Daniel a new shirt by the end of the week. Do we understand each other?"

Maxie couldn't speak. This was just too good to be true!

Mr. Shivers stood up and pointed toward the waiting room. "You can go now, Mr. Zuckerman. On your way, could you please send in Miss Swanson?"

Maxie practically ran out the door. Rosie and Earl looked up at him. Their faces were green almost. He *had* to find a way to let them know that

Mr. Jim hadn't squealed. Otherwise, one of them would spill the beans for sure.

But how? Mr. Shivers could hear every word he said. Plus, nosy Mrs. Trumbull was staring over the counter at him.

Maxie plastered a smile on his face and wiped his forehead. "Whew!" he said, hoping his relief would be a hint.

Earl thought it meant that Maxie was sweaty.

He nodded in agreement. "Yeah. Whew," he repeated sickly.

Think, Maxie! Think! Think! he ordered his brain.

"Mr. Shivers wants to see you next," he told Rosie. Then he cupped his hands around his mouth, and as softy as he could, he whispered, "He...doesn't...know."

Rosie raised her eyebrows. "Huh? Who? What?" she asked.

Maxie started to panic. If only they had a secret code! If only there was some secret way to tell Rosie she was safe! Then—out of the blue—it hit him!

The all-clear signal! Of *course!*

Quickly, Maxie began to swing his arm in big, wide circles all around his body.

Please, Rosie! he begged in his head. Please understand! It's the all-clear signal! We're off the hook!

By this time, Maxie's arm was circling his body so fast that he thought it would fly right off his shoulder. He was still praying for another miracle when he heard Mr. Shivers' voice behind him.

"Mr. Zuckerman? What are you doing, son? Trying to bring a plane in for a landing?"

A light went on in Rosie's head, and she nodded.

Quickly, she poked Earl with her elbow, and he nodded, too.

Relief flooded over them.

They were safe.

9 THUMBS UP

Earl was the last one back to the swing set that morning. Maxie and Rosie were sure that he had understood the all-clear signal. But still, it was nerve-wracking waiting for him.

When they finally saw him walking across the grass, they ran to meet him.

"Well?" asked Rosie. "What happened? Tell us, Earl! Everything's okay, right? You didn't mention the Dumpster, did you? Come on! What did Mr. Shivers say?"

Earl crossed his arms and looked annoyed. "He said I had to read out loud. That's what he said."

"Yeah, fine. But that's *all* he said, right?" Maxie asked him.

"No," said Earl. "He also said that reading is

fundamental. And that I'm not allowed to say no to my teacher. And that from now on I have to try to—"

Rosie grabbed Earl by the shirt. "For gosh sake, Earl! Just tell us! Did you mention the Dumpster or not?"

Earl pulled a Kleenex out of his shirt pocket and wiped his top lip. "Not," he said.

Maxie started jumping up and down. "I can't believe it! This is amazing! We actually got away with it! We ditched school, and we didn't get caught!"

Rosie didn't look sure. "I don't know, Max. Do you really, really think that it's over?"

"Yeah," said Earl. "I mean why didn't Mr. Jim tell on us? It just doesn't make sense to me."

Maxie was still jumping around. "Who knows? Who cares? The important thing is that he *didn't*."

"Not *yet*, you mean," said Rosie.

"Exactly," said Earl. "Maybe he just hasn't gotten around to it. Same thing for that little girl, too. Just because she hasn't told anyone yet doesn't mean she won't."

Maxie put his hands over his ears. "Stop it, you two. I mean it! You guys are like the Gloom and Doom twins. It's over, I'm telling you. Mr. Jim didn't squeal. And the little kindergarten dipsey got scared away by a threat from the bogeyman. We *did* it. You can relax. Nothing is going to happen."

Rosie and Earl looked at each other. It was reassuring to hear the confidence in Maxie's voice.

"Well…maybe," said Rosie.

"Yeah…maybe," echoed Earl.

Just then, the school door opened, and Mr. Jim headed toward the playground with his weed trimmer.

Maxie Zuckerman was the first to cover his face.

When the bell finally rang, Rosie left the playground in a hurry. But instead of taking her usual route to her classroom, she hurried down the hall and waited near the kindergarten. Sometimes the only way to be sure something was done right was to do it yourself.

Outside the classroom, several little girls were lining up to go inside. One was skipping all around in circles. She was wearing a name tag on her dress. It read: Emily Sweete.

Rosie went over and tapped her on the shoulder. "Could I talk to you a minute, Emily?"

Emily Sweete smoothed out her hair. "Who are you?"

Rosie bent down. "I'm a friend of those two boys you saw in the hall on Friday. Remember those two boys?"

Emily nodded cutely. "You mean Ted and the skinny boy?"

"Yes. Right. Ted and the skinny boy. I was just wondering if you told anybody about them. Like about how they sort of magically vanished while they were watching you skip?"

Emily put her hands on her hips. "They didn't magically vanish," she said. "They went right out the door before school was over. I saw them."

Rosie tensed. "Yeah, well, whatever. The point is, you didn't *tell* anyone about them, right?"

Emily Sweete looked all around. Then she cupped her hands around Rosie's ear and whispered. "No. 'Cause guess why? The cookie man called me at my house. And he said not to talk about those boys."

Rosie gave her a funny look. "The *cookie* man?"

"Yes," said Emily. "He said not to tell on those guys or else he'd come visit me. He didn't sound that friendly."

She frowned. "What does the cookie man do, anyway? Does he come to your house and eat all your cookies?"

Rosie tried not to smile. "Yes, Emily," she said seriously. "Yes, he does. He comes to your house and he eats all your cookies."

She covered her mouth and grinned. Poor Earl Wilber. Who else could pretend to be the *bogeyman* and end up as the *cookie* man?

Feeling a little better, Rosie looked around. She didn't have much time left, but there was someone else she really wanted to find.

"Emily, do you remember the fire drill we had on Friday? You didn't happen to see a boy kicking the Dumpster while we were outside, did you? I'm pretty sure it was a kindergarten boy."

Emily Sweete's face lit right up. She pointed to a curly-headed boy at the end of the hall. "Him! Him! It was Arnie Schwartz! Arnie Schwartz kicks everything!"

Rosie looked down the hall. Arnie Schwartz, she thought. What do you know...I found you.

She thanked Emily and gave her a hug. Five was such a great age. No one loved to tattle better than five-year-olds.

Too bad that most of them outgrew it.

When Rosie got back to her room, she pulled her yellow notepad from her desk. Quickly, she began to write:

Dear Kindergarten Teacher,
Arnold Schwartz was kicking the Dumpster during the fire drill on Friday. He didn't get caught, but it's not too late to speak to him about this.

Kicking and denting public
property are against the law.

Rosie stopped and looked down at what she'd
written. She read it over and over. Something didn't
sound right, but she wasn't sure what. She thought
and thought. Then slowly, it became clearer.

She picked up her pencil again.

Dear Kindergarten Teacher,
Arnold Schwartz was kicking the
Dumpster during the fire drill on
Friday. He didn't get caught. But it's
not too late to speak to him about
this. Kicking the Dumpster is so in
considerate. If people are hiding in
the Dumpster waiting to ditch school,
loud kicking can give them a headache.

Rosie reread the note one last time. If you
were going to be a tattletale, it was only fair to
include all the facts.

She stuck the yellow pad back into her desk.

When the bell rang for recess, she slipped it into her back pocket and hustled outside.

The Dumpster was at the very end of the parking lot. Rosie hurried down there and ripped the note about Arnie Schwartz off her pad. After taking one last look at it, she wadded it up and sent it sailing over the side of the big can.

A few seconds later, her yellow notepad came sailing in behind it.

When Maxie walked into his classroom, Mrs. Trout wasn't there yet. Daniel W. was, though. Daniel had gotten there early just to wait for Maxie.

As soon as Maxie sat down, Daniel W. was all over him. "You owe me a shirt, Zuckerman," he said. "I want the exact same kind, too. I mean it. The exact same green-and-brown camouflage T-shirt as the one you ruined."

Maxie smiled. After all the stress of the weekend, Daniel's stupid army T-shirt hardly seemed important. "What if I just buy a white T-shirt and let something green and brown throw up on it?" he suggested.

99

Daniel W. was just about to grab Maxie by the collar when Mrs. Trout walked into the room.

"Problem, gentlemen?" she asked.

Daniel raised his hand. "Tell him he has to buy me the exact same shirt, Mrs. Trout. Tell him!"

"I think that's already understood, isn't it, Maxie?" she asked.

Maxie nodded. "Yes, ma'am. Yes, it is," he said.

Just then, there was a light knock on the door. When Maxie looked up, he saw Mr. Foote, the music teacher, wheeling in his portable keyboard. Just like Mr. Bucky, Mr. Foote had lost his own classroom last year. But unlike Mr. Bucky, Mr. Foote was almost always in a good mood.

He hummed as he lifted a big cardboard box from the top of the keyboard and began passing out wood blocks and drumsticks. Babyish or not, Mr. Foote believed in teaching his students timing, beat, and rhythm.

Unfortunately, there were never enough drumsticks to go around. So, unless someone was absent, Maxie almost always had to play his wood block with a wooden spoon from the cafeteria.

This time, when Mr. Foote got to Maxie's desk, they both looked down in the box. "Gee, what do you know? I get the wooden spoon again," said Maxie.

Mr. Foote smiled. "Wood is wood," he replied, and he went back to the front.

Daniel W. spun around and laughed in his face. "Look on the bright side. You're the only one in the room who can play your instrument and eat a bowl of soup at the same time."

In the front of the room, Mr. Foote was passing out songbooks.

"Today, we're going to finish learning all the verses to 'Home on the Range,'" he said. "If we tap rhythmically on our wood blocks, we can make them sound like horses' hooves clopping across the desert."

There were moans and groans from all parts of the room, but Mr. Foote ignored them.

"Page thirty-four, please." After that, he stood at his keyboard and held his hands in the air like a conductor.

Daniel W. turned around again. "Hey, Zuckerman? You got your spoon ready?" he asked loudly.

The kids in front of him looked back and started to grin. More than anything, Maxie wished he didn't have to look at their faces.

Then, all of a sudden, he remembered something he'd learned in the Dumpster. If you really, really, really didn't want to see something, just don't look.

He lowered his eyes. There! Now he couldn't see anyone at all. And even better, as he was looking down at his own desktop, he caught sight of his lunch sack sticking out of his desk.

Maxie began to smile. Maybe Daniel W. was right. Maybe this old wooden spoon had more than one purpose.

As his classmates held out their instruments and got ready to sing, Maxie Zuckerman snuck his hand into his desk and opened the top of his lunch sack.

"Aaaaaand begin!" said Mr. Foote, getting them started.

All over the room, kids began keeping time to the tune.

> Oh, give me a hooooome,
> Where the buffalo roooooam,
> And the deer and the antelope plaaaaaaay.

Keeping an eye on the music teacher, Maxie pretended to sing along with the others. Then, as soon as Mr. Foote wasn't looking, he carefully pulled the chocolate pudding cup out of his lunch bag.

> Where seldom is hearrrrrrrd,
> A discouraging worrrrrd...

By the time his class had finished the song, Maxie Zuckerman had finished his pudding.

He smacked his lips and put down the spoon.

Earl Wilber's class had PE at 10:15. Today, Ms. Garcia was making them play kickball. Earl was in the outfield. He hated being in the outfield. It was boring and hot, and nothing ever came to him.

The other team had been up forever, it seemed. Earl Wilber squatted down in the grass. When Ms. Garcia didn't tell him to stand up again, he sat down all the way.

That's when he heard it. A loud buzzing sound had started up behind him. What was that noise? It sounded so familiar. It sounded like a...a weed trimmer.

Earl turned. Oh no! It was Mr. Jim! He was trimming the weeds in the outfield not far from where Earl sat!

In a flash, Earl pulled his mother's huge sunglasses out of his pocket and shoved them on his face. This was the moment he'd been dreading. If Mr. Jim recognized his face, he'd turn him in to Mr. Shivers for sure!

Earl had to get out of the outfield! He stood up and waved his hand in the air for Ms. Garcia to see. He'd tell her he had to go to the bathroom. He'd tell her he was sick. Anything to get him away from Mr. Jim!

But luck was not on Earl's side. Before Ms. Garcia could see him, Rodney Russell Rodgers came up to the plate and kicked the ball right over the head of the second baseman.

Earl gulped. The ball was rolling straight toward him! Everyone was watching.

"Get it, Earl! Get the ball!" they screamed from all over the field. "Hurry! Hurry! Run! Run!"

Just then, the weed trimmer stopped buzzing. Mr. Jim was watching, too. Earl could feel his eyes on his back.

But no matter what, he *had* to get the ball. He couldn't look like a doofus in front of his class. Not again. So keeping his head down, he chased it directly past Mr. Jim.

He picked it up and hurled it back with all his might.

For once, it went in the right direction! Earl's class started to clap. Rodney Russell Rodgers was out at home!

It should have been a nice moment. But Earl could still feel Mr. Jim looking at him.

When would this ever be over? Hadn't they been punished enough for ditching school? Did the stress have to go on forever?

Suddenly, without even thinking about it, Earl took off his sunglasses and looked straight at the custodian.

"We made a mistake, okay?" he said. "I mean, geez, everybody does the wrong thing sometimes. Even you, I bet. Haven't you ever done the wrong thing, Mr. Jim? Huh? Haven't you ever made a mistake?"

Mr. Jim didn't say a word. Instead, he reached down to start the weed trimmer again. But right before he did, just a hint of a smile showed on his face. "Yep" was all he said.

Then he looked up at Earl and winked.

Stunned, Earl stood there for a second. Then finally, he wiped his sweaty palms on his pants. And he winked back.

Maxie was waiting at the swings after school. He didn't know if the others would show up. They hadn't planned to meet or anything. But for some reason, he thought they would come.

Rosie spotted him on her way out of the gate. Earl did, too.

As the three of them hurried toward each other, Maxie gave them a thumbs-up. Rosie grinned and gave him the all-clear signal. Earl made the "okay" sign with his finger and thumb.

As soon as they got close enough, everyone began talking at once. Rosie gave them the good news about Emily Sweete and how she wasn't going to tell. Earl told them about his run-in with Mr. Jim. Maxie talked about music class. There was still pudding on his lip.

They started to laugh. Earl and Rosie high-fived. Maxie and Rosie low-fived. When Earl tried to put on his sunglasses again, Maxie jumped on his back and wrestled him to the ground. Rosie piled on top of them.

Suddenly, they felt like best friends.

They looked at each other and smiled.

Yeah. Just maybe they were.

Maxie's Words

dipsey (DIP-see)—a sinker for a fishing line
  (p. 94)
foozle (FOO-zul)—fumble (p. 74)
fub (fub)—cheat; trick (p. 74)
fuff (fuf)—puff (p. 33)
mungo (MUNG-go)—the waste produced from
  hard-spun or felted cloth (p. 40)
niblick (NIB-lick)—a golf club with a slanted iron
  head for lifting the ball out of bunkers,
  long grass, etc. (p. 25)
slub (slub)—a slightly twisted roll of cotton, wool,
  or silk (p. 49)

Barbara Park is one of today's funniest, most popular writers for middle-graders. Her novels, which include *Skinnybones, The Kid in the Red Jacket, Rosie Swanson: Fourth-Grade Geek for President,* and *Dear God, Help!!! Love, Earl,* have won just about every award given by children.

She has also created the Junie B. Jones character for the Random House Stepping Stone Books list. Recent books about Junie include *Junie B. Jones Is (almost) a Flower Girl, Junie B. Jones and the Mushy Gushy Valentime,* and *Junie B. Jones Has a Peep in Her Pocket.*

Ms. Park earned a B.S. degree in education at the University of Alabama and lives in Scottsdale, Arizona, with her husband.